He

Pepe's Dog

Scripture Union

Other books by the same author
Caleb's lamb – Tiger series
If only – Leopard series

© Helen Santos 1996
First published 1996

Scripture Union, 207–209 Queensway, Bletchley,
Milton Keynes, MK2 2EB, England.

ISBN 1 85999 041 X

British Library Cataloguing-in-Publication Data.
A catalogue record of this book is available from the
British Library.

Phototypeset by Intype, London.
Printed and bound in Great Britain by Cox & Wyman
Ltd, Reading.

The story is about a boy who lives in Spain. He is called **Pepe**. His name sounds like 'peppay'.

There are a few Spanish words in the story. Here is a list of some of the Spanish words and a guide to how to say them:

perro you say 'perro' (which means dog)

feliz you say 'felith' (which means happy)

hermoso you say 'airmoso' (which means beautiful)

jefe you say 'hefay' (which means boss)

Café Playa you say 'Café Plya' (which means The Beach Café)

Dios te ama you say 'Deeos tayama' (which means God loves you)

muy grande you say 'mooy granday' (which means very big)

Como tu llamar? you say 'Como tuyamar?' (which means, What do you call them?)

Chapter one

Pepe believed in miracles. He'd lived all his nine years among people who believed in miracles so, to him, a miracle was no more unexpected than the annual October rains. The fact that the October rains sometimes failed (and the spring rains, too) didn't mean that it would never rain again. It just meant they had been delayed. Sooner or later it would rain and every cloud, however small, was a hopeful reminder.

Pepe was sitting at one of the shabby green metal tables outside his home. His home was called 'Café Playa' (The Beach Café) because it was right on the beach, all by itself. Behind it was a high, sheltering sand-dune. In front, was the Atlantic Ocean with the North African coast about a hundred miles away.

He was looking at his favourite book. It was December and, although the sky was blue, a gusty wind was fighting to snatch the book away from him. It whipped the pages over in a rush, faster than his hands could hold them still.

As it wasn't a story book it didn't matter. The glossy pages were full of photos of dogs. Pepe's twenty-year old brother, Big Pepe, had given him the book for his birthday back in the summer. It was the only book he owned if you didn't count his school books.

By now he knew every picture by heart, even though there were hundreds of them. If he'd ever gone to a dog show – which was unlikely because dog shows didn't happen in his part of the world – he would have recognised every single breed.

Pepe was amazed at all the different sorts of dogs there were. Where he lived most people had mongrels, and most of them were small and fat, with bulging eyes and flat snuffly noses.

Pepe had wanted a dog of his own ever since he'd seen a 'Lassie' film on television. He didn't want just any old dog. He wanted one that could open doors, jump through hoops of fire, carry parcels, rescue drowning people, understand everything he said and almost talk. Just like Lassie.

'You don't want a dog!' exclaimed Big Pepe with a laugh. 'You want a dream.'

'A lady in the church – her little dog's just had puppies,' said his mother. 'You can have one of them.'

'You mean the lady with blue hair?' asked Pepe cautiously.

'She hasn't got blue hair. It's just that the hairdresser got the colour too strong.'

'It's blue,' insisted Pepe, an impish look in his black eyes. 'And I don't want one of her puppies. They'll be as ugly as their mother, with bandy legs.'

'All the dogs round here have bandy legs,' laughed his father. 'What do you expect?'

'A proper dog,' said Pepe with dignity, 'or none at all.'

6

So, instead of a bandy-legged puppy, he was given a book for his birthday. Opening it was like going through a door into a different world. He liked the book so much that he even slept with it in his arms.

His delight made everyone happy and Pepe became what his father called, 'a connoisseur'.

'What's that?' he demanded.

'Someone who's seen the best and is spoilt for anything else.'

'Is that bad or good?' wondered Pepe, not sure if he was being made fun of. He was often teased.

'I don't know,' admitted his father. 'It depends on what you want.'

After Pepe had gone through the book dozens of times he knew exactly which dog he wanted – an Irish Setter. The gloss of that particular page was wearing thin because of the many times his fingertips had traced over every part of the photo.

He knew every wave of its rich red coat. He had kissed the black nose a hundred times. He could almost feel the softness of those long, drooping ears. He couldn't put into words what he felt when he looked at that noble, almost golden-coloured dog. But one thing he knew – if he couldn't have an Irish Setter there wasn't a single dog in the world that he wanted.

Once Pepe was absolutely certain of this, he knew what to do. He had to tell Jesus about it, though he reckoned Jesus must know already because he always knew everything. He knew when people were happy or sad. He knew when they got mad about things. He knew what they wanted.

His parents and the Junior Church teacher had said that Jesus didn't always give you what you wanted. He gave you what you needed, which wasn't always the same thing. So, for a while, Pepe had held back before asking Jesus for an Irish Setter. Did he really need one?

Pretty soon he decided that he did. He needed a friend, just like that boy in the 'Lassie' film. He didn't have a special friend of his own age. The one boy in his class who wanted to be his friend wasn't allowed to play with him because he was a Christian. A lot of the boys were unfriendly because he was half-gypsy. Except for the twins, Victor and David, the church children were either older or younger than he was. The twins didn't want to be friends and were bullies when no one was watching.

If he had a dog it wouldn't matter about not having a special friend.

His parents had been ready to get him one for his birthday so there'd surely be no trouble about having one for 'Kings'* instead. That wasn't the difficult part.

Pepe had never seen a real Irish Setter. There were none in the town. It wasn't even a Spanish dog, unlike some of them in the book. Were there any Irish Setters in Spain? Or would you have to go all the way to Ireland (wherever that was) to find one?

When doubt began to cloud his hopes, that's

---

* Spanish children get their Christmas presents from the 'wise men or kings', not from Father Christmas, on the sixth of January. The day is known as 'Reyes' (Kings).

when Pepe just knew in his heart there would be a miracle.

So he prayed one day while he was standing at the edge of the sea, watching the foam come right up to the tips of his trainers but no further. He was wondering why the sea always stopped where it did, why it didn't rush over everything and flood the whole world.

He remembered that God had made the sea and given it a stopping place. His father had told him that when, one stormy night, he'd been scared that their little home on the beach would be washed away. They'd all prayed that the waves would obey the voice of the Lord and stay where they belonged – and they did. All the same, it had been a scary night.

'Lord Jesus,' he said, while watching the ebb and flow of the ocean, 'please help my father get me an Irish Setter like the one in my book. I really need one. Amen.'

Then he added a, 'thank you,' because he knew that, sooner or later, the dog would be his. He didn't worry about how. Jesus would take care of that side of things. But from that day on he was sure in his heart about it.

He was remembering his prayer that gusty December day, when he had no playmate but the wind and the dog of his dreams. He liked to pretend the dog was already there, keeping him company. But his imagination didn't run very far because he'd never had a dog. What did dogs do when they weren't rescuing people or jumping through fire?

At that moment their only winter customer turned up. She sat herself at a table as far from Pepe as she could and nodded in reply to his instant, ' 'Allo,' in English. Then she looked at the sea, which pounded on the shore that day, as wild as the wind.

Pepe wasn't surprised to see her. Every day she passed his home on her morning walk and on the way back she would stop for a glass of hot mint tea.

'You can set your clock by her!' his father had admiringly exclaimed, though he didn't do it. The big tin alarm clock at his parents' bedside was silent as often as it was ticking.

'She's a lady,' he had also said with equal admiration, though he didn't explain how you could tell.

He liked serving her. He practised his English with her and Pepe was proud to know how clever his father was. Pepe was learning English at school but he'd never tried saying more than, 'hello,' to her. He decided to show her his dog book and practise his English, too.

'You want look?' he confidently asked as he pulled up a chair beside her, placing the book on the table in an important way. He wasn't put off when she didn't answer. Everyone knew that English people love dogs.

Proudly, Pepe turned the pages, pointing at the photos and looking with a hopeful smile for her reaction. He knew the limits of his English. Besides, the pictures said everything.

After a while, she began to take notice. She didn't have much choice. Who could resist Pepe's shining enthusiasm as Dalmatians and Labradors, huskies and whippets, bulldogs and Jack Russells were unfolded before them?

'Nice,' she started saying in Spanish. '*Simpático . . . Bonito . . .*' And, '*Muy grande.*'

When she repeated the same words in English, Pepe copied her

'Nice. Pretty. Very big.' Only his, 'very big' came out, 'bery vig.'

Just then his father appeared, knowing it was about time for his only customer. He greeted her with his usual big smile and made as if to chase Pepe and his book away.

'Don't bother the lady!' he exclaimed. 'She's not interested in your dogs.'

The lady managed to work out what he was saying. '*Esta bien. No molesta. Libro bonito,*' she replied. 'It's all right. He's not bothering me. It's a lovely book.' (At least that's what she tried to say.)

So while his father returned indoors to make the one and only drink he would sell that day, Pepe drew her back to the book. He had been saving the dog of his dreams till last.

Chapter two

Very few people in that coastal town in the far south of Spain knew anything about Miss Beamish. They knew how much she paid for the little house she'd rented in a narrow cobbled street just off the main square. But why she'd chosen their town to live in, or how long she planned to stay, was a mystery.

They were used to foreign holiday-makers and the occasional lone writer or artist, but Miss Beamish was none of these. She made no effort to make friends with anyone so gossip had to be invented. She was obviously 'odd', with all her walking and swimming when the season was over. The grandmothers were shocked by her winter swimming but the young people laughed.

They all said, 'What else do you expect of a foreigner? Their ways are not like ours.'

Pepe's family knew more about Miss Beamish than most people because all through the summer she bought a cold drink after her morning dip in the sea. Then she would sit in the shade of the thatched extension of The Beach Café, always alone though surrounded by people. There was no other shade on that beach.

After a while Miss Beamish discovered that the best time to be on the beach in summer was when the sun had set. The night had a gentler heat; the sea had a mysterious calm, awash with moonlight; chattering voices lost their harshness; and the red, yellow, blue and green light-bulbs dangling from the thatch gave a welcoming glow. There was fresh fried fish and sand-cooled water melons on the menu at night and Pepe was still serving customers alongside his father.

He looked like a real waiter as he squeezed between people and tables, bringing full dishes, collecting empty ones and taking orders. Miss Beamish knew nothing about boys but something in her heart was touched by his black curls and merry dark eyes.

By the end of August all the Spanish families had gone and, by the end of September, most of the foreign holiday-makers, too. The coloured lights were taken down and packed in a box but, because The Beach Café was also a home, no shutters went up and the door wasn't locked. The tables and chairs were left outside as there was nowhere else to put them. Apart from Pepe's family – and a few horseriders who galloped by without stopping – Miss Beamish was the only person to be seen on that stretch of beach in winter.

'She's a lonely lady,' decided Pepe's father after noticing her solitary figure day after day.

Pepe's mother had been lonely for many years before she became a Christian. She sighed as she said, 'Being lonely is one of the worst things. She's old, too.'

13

'And a foreigner,' added Big Pepe.

'Doesn't the Lord want us to be especially kind to foreigners?' asked Maria. 'Something about his people having been slaves and foreigners? He knows how miserable that can make you.'

'It's in the Bible,' agreed her husband, José.

So the next day he had waited for Miss Beamish to come back from her walk, patiently watching out for her. He waved her towards a table, making signs for her to stop and have something to drink.

'I think you closed,' Miss Beamish told him, trying out the Spanish she was slowly learning with the help of books and cassettes.

'For you, nice English lady, we always open,' he replied in English. She knew he meant it.

Miss Beamish soon discovered that José didn't know how to make proper English tea, not even with a tea bag. So, she got used to drinking mint tea instead. She never went into the café, preferring to sit watching the sea. José knew she liked to be alone so, after just a few words, he would go away.

While he chatted to Miss Beamish, Maria would say a brief prayer, 'Lord, make the English lady more friendly.' Then she would eagerly ask him, 'Well, how is she today?'

'The same,' he always replied with a shrug. But it was a hopeful sort of shrug.

If Jesus wanted to reach the English lady's heart through hot mint tea and their prayers somehow he would do it. So José was very pleased when he discovered Pepe and Miss Beamish with their heads together over the dog book, although he pretended not to be.

14

'Our son is making friends with the English lady,' he exclaimed to his wife as he looked for a tea bag, a glass and a saucer. 'It's the dog. You know how the English like dogs.'

Maria took a little peep from the doorway. She didn't want to spoil anything. Besides, she felt very shy of Miss Beamish even though she often prayed for her. She very rarely went outside to customers. Her job was behind the counter, selling cold drinks in summer and washing dishes all the year round.

She swelled with pride and a smile creased her plump cheeks. Then she slipped back indoors, not wanting Pepe to see her. But she peeped out from time to time, making her husband laugh.

She saw Pepe turn to his favourite page. He smoothed his hands over it in a dramatic way and waited for Miss Beamish to say something. Miss Beamish might know nothing about boys; she might want to keep herself to herself; but the silence and the look – and the way Pepe's fingers gently touched the dog's muzzle – said more than any amount of words in any language.

Carefully she put together a sentence in Spanish. '*Esto es un perro hermoso*,' which means, 'This is a beautiful dog.'

An enormous grin lit up his face and an extra sparkle came to his eyes. With great faith, he announced in English, 'This . . .' He pointed to the Setter. 'This. My.' He pointed to himself to make quite sure she understood.

She didn't. Was he telling her that this was his favourite picture? Was he telling her that he had a dog like that? Miss Beamish had only ever seen a

15

few wild cats near The Beach Café, crunching ravenously through fish bones.

Pepe tried again, 'My dog. Tomorrow.' His face screwed up with the effort. He wanted to say, 'one day' but could only think of, 'tomorrow'.

'You're going to have a dog like this tomorrow!' exclaimed Miss Beamish, forgetting that Pepe's English was probably worse than her Spanish.

'My father. He give,' Pepe went on, not put off by so many words which he didn't understand.

He hugged the book against his chest, still open at the precious page. He wanted to show the English lady how much he was going to love this dog when it was his.

Miss Beamish was still struggling to understand. She knew very little about the family at The Beach Café but they looked rather poor. Even in England, a pedigree dog would cost a lot of money. How much more would such a dog cost in Spain? Still, it was none of her business.

At that point, Pepe saw his father at the door. He ran and grabbed his hand, pulling him over to the table.

'Tell her, tell her,' he demanded. 'Tell her about my dog.'

'One day, I get dog for him,' José said.

'This one?' Miss Beamish couldn't keep the surprise from her voice.

José shrugged his shoulders. Then, cupping his hands as if holding something small, he went on, 'I bring little dog. He happy.'

'What are you telling her?' Pepe asked.

'That I'm going to bring you a puppy.'

16

'This one,' he insisted. 'I only want this one.'

José stretched out his hand and ruffled his son's hair. 'We'll see,' he said. 'We'll see.'

Chapter three

Big Pepe was called Big Pepe because he had the same name as his brother. Their proper names were José, just like their father, so there were three Josés in the same family. Nearly every José has the nickname 'Pepe', but it isn't very usual for two brothers to share the same name.

In fact, the two Pepes were only half-brothers. José's first wife had died when Big Pepe was quite small and they had gone through some hard times, both together and apart. José travelled all over the country, looking for work. Sometimes he mixed cement and carried bricks on a building site; sometimes he worked long hours in hotels and cafés. He picked cotton, harvested potatoes and pruned peach trees.

None of these jobs lasted for long and it was very hard for him to look after his son when he moved around so much. So Big Pepe spent much of his life in different children's homes. In some of the places he was ill-treated. In all of them he was a nobody. He had no memory at all of his mother. His days were spent either longing to be with his father or – when he was with him – fearfully dreading the next goodbye.

One day, his father met some Christians who invited him along to their meetings. José still enjoyed talking about those days.

'I thought they were crazy people. They were as poor as I was, some even poorer. And if I had problems, some of them had bigger ones. But they were all so happy. Nothing could stop them praising God.'

The tears would still come to his eyes as he remembered how they opened their hearts, and their homes, to him and his son.

'I knew nothing about Jesus till I met those people,' he would say, 'but when I saw Jesus in them I knew he was real.'

Among them was a Gypsy called Maria. She was a widow and had no children. One of the worst things for a Gypsy woman is to have no children. She had brought a curse on herself for marrying a non-Gypsy, her family told her, and they didn't want her back.

Someone had told her how Jesus cared about outcasts. The Bible was full of stories about women that Jesus helped. Because she couldn't read, she listened hungrily to every sermon and remembered them all. She discovered that God knew exactly how she felt about being childless and alone.

'Then miracles started to happen,' was the only way Maria could explain it after she became a Christian.

She got to know José – they were baptised in the sea on the same day – and eventually they were married. Suddenly, she had a son as well as a husband.

At first, Big Pepe found it hard to call her

'Mama', not because he didn't want to but because the word was so strange to him. He was painfully shy, too, until she took him into her plump arms and lavished her hungry love on him. The first time he called her 'Mama', her black eyes filled with tears which splashed all over him as she showered his face with kisses. Then they both laughed and hugged each other and it was as if they'd always been a family.

Soon, an even bigger miracle happened. In spite of everyone thinking it was quite impossible, José's second son was born. Nothing in the world could stop Maria giving this child his father's name. When he began to talk, he was the one who gave his half-brother the title 'Big Pepe'.

It would have been very easy for Big Pepe to be jealous of his brother. He was so spoilt and adored. But even Big Pepe was awed by the miracle of his birth. So often he'd longed for a brother or sister – someone to call his own – and this baby was his as much as anyone else's.

As for José, he was determined to give his new family a more secure life. He heard about the empty house on the beach, got permission to turn it into a café, and he and Maria pooled their savings to buy it. They had to move away from the place where God had so greatly blessed them, and José still had to do extra work when he could find it, but nothing could spoil their joy. They even found the small church that they'd prayed for. No wonder they believed in miracles.

Money was scarce but love was plentiful. This was just as well because The Beach Café was very small and they could have spent all their time arguing. Most of their life was carried on outdoors, where Pepe had all the freedom of the beach as well as the sound of the sea to lull him to sleep at night.

For the last two summers, Pepe had helped serve their customers. It was like a game to him, even though he had to work as hard as everyone else. His father couldn't afford to pay someone to help him when they were busy. So Pepe was given the grand title, *Camarero* (waiter), while the Spanish customers called his father, *Jefe* (boss).

He had learnt to be careful of hot plates. He no longer broke more than a glass or two. And he was proud to hear his father say at the end of the long day – perhaps at two or three o'clock in the morning – 'I wouldn't have been able to manage without him.'

The customers spoiled him almost as much as his own family did, so Pepe had never known fear and loneliness as Big Pepe had. But he still wanted a friend who wouldn't mind him being a Gypsy and a Christian. He was quite sure that dogs didn't worry about things like that.

Pepe didn't keep on at his parents about the Irish Setter. He knew they would have brought him one the next day if they could. He had learnt from his parents to leave things with the Lord. He believed and waited.

Meanwhile, José, Maria and Big Pepe secretly discussed how they could find such a dog for him, and by the sixth of January, the twelfth day of Christmas.

'The English lady will help us,' decided José when they couldn't think of anything. 'Everyone

21

knows the English love dogs. She will know what to do.'

So it was that one morning, while Pepe was at school, his father decided to talk to Miss Beamish. He was very nervous. Would his English be good enough, or her Spanish? Would she be offended? She was such a hard person to get to know.

Before she came they all prayed.

'Please help José to know how to explain,' prayed Maria.

'Please don't let her be angry and stop coming,' prayed José.

Big Pepe couldn't really believe that the English lady could possibly find an Irish Setter puppy in time, so his prayer was, 'Lord, we need a miracle. Nothing is too small or unimportant for you.'

When José insisted that Miss Beamish should come inside the café that morning for her glass of mint tea, she knew it was no ordinary occasion. She had never been inside The Beach Café before and was surprised at how small it was. Besides the counter, there was only room for two small tables and six chairs, just like the ones outside.

When José, having brought the tea, sat himself at the same table, Miss Beamish was mystified as well as a little nervous. Suddenly, Maria appeared in the doorway that led to the kitchen. Even though she didn't know any English, she wanted to watch and listen.

Maria was round and wide enough to fill the doorway and her smile was as lovely as Pepe's. José was only about half her width, thin, wiry and not very tall. His dark hair was grizzled and his face was full of creases from many years of working under a strong sun.

In a mixture of English and Spanish, José told Miss Beamish what they wanted, while Maria nodded her head, enjoying every minute. She was proud of her husband, who could speak two languages so well.

Miss Beamish was so taken aback by his request that she didn't know what to say. 'But Christmas is only two weeks away,' was all she came out with.

'No, no. Here, January six,' said José, as if those extra twelve days made all the difference, as if they made his request reasonable.

Miss Beamish nodded, then realised her mistake when a big smile broke over his earnest face. He thought she was saying yes.

'No!' she cried. 'Not enough time. Impossible . . . *Imposible! No tiempo!*' she exclaimed again in Spanish, to make sure he understood.

Even that was a mistake. It make it look as though she could do it if she had more time.

'No impossible,' was José's optimistic reply. 'You try.'

She could see there was no way of convincing him. He had made up his mind. Before, he'd been planning to get Pepe a mongrel. Now it had to be an Irish Setter. The whole idea was ridiculous. What did he expect her to do?

She wanted to feel angry. They had no right to involve her in their problems. But even as she tried to think of a simple way of explaining this, José

went on, 'I know expensive. Good dog. Not . . .
You know. Not . . .'

He used his hands so expressively, showing
shapes and sizes all rolled together, that Miss
Beamish soon guessed what he was trying to say.
'Mongrel?' she helped him.

Maria, in the doorway, burst out laughing.

'Couldn't you just get him a mongrel?' Miss
Beamish pleaded.

José firmly shook his head. 'He want this dog.
Special dog. You understand?'

He pulled a wad of banknotes out of his pocket
and pushed them towards her. Miss Beamish
shook her head.

'I don't know how much it will cost. I don't think
it's possible. Please . . . *Por favor* . . .'

'You try. You do,' encouraged José with the
same winning smile that Pepe used so often. 'You
clever lady.'

At that, even Miss Beamish had to smile, and
then they all began to laugh. It was so ridiculous
and yet she knew that somehow they'd managed
to persuade her – at least to try.

At this point Big Pepe appeared behind his
mother.

'Come here. Come here!' José shouted, beckon-
ing to an empty chair. 'This my son, too,' he
explained proudly to Miss Beamish. 'You not
know?'

How could she know? Big Pepe was a very
shy person. He preferred staying in the kitchen,
cooking, to serving and talking to customers. However, apart from being a head taller, Big Pepe and
José did look alike. They had the same fine nose,

24

clear brown eyes and straight eyebrows. He didn't look a bit like his brother.

Very formally, he and Miss Beamish shook hands. They were both equally shy. At last, Maria found the courage to come closer, though she didn't sit down. It was a very special and exciting occasion for them. Miss Beamish's heart sank.

She didn't believe in miracles. She didn't even believe in God.

Chapter four

Miss Beamish went back to her little house feeling very cross. How had The Beach Café family managed to involve her in Pepe's fantasy? Even worse, how had she let herself become involved? All her life she'd managed to keep herself to herself and she was too old to change. But she also prided herself on being a person who kept her word, who wouldn't fail in what she set out to do. Like it or not, she had agreed to do *something*!

By the time she'd prepared her lunch, eaten it and washed up, she had a sensible idea. The best and proper thing any British person abroad should do if they had a problem was to get in touch with the British consul. So she wrote a letter, asking if they could tell her how she could buy an Irish Setter in Spain. Then she began to wonder how long it would take them to get the letter. If it only arrived just before Christmas, by the time they replied it would be too late for 'Kings'.

In the end, she decided she would try telephoning the consul. At least she'd get an immediate reply. Miss Beamish didn't have a telephone. There was no one she needed to talk to, nor anyone who would want to ring her. So the next morning, she went to *La Telefónica* (the Telephone Exchange) which was next to the baker's, in the main square.

There were two glass cabins, each with a telephone on a shelf and a round black stool; and there was a counter, behind which the lady in charge had a switchboard. It was old-fashioned but it worked. You gave her the telephone number and she would make the call. She then told you to go to Cabin One or Two, where she would connect you. Afterwards, she told you how much it cost.

Miss Beamish's call wasn't satisfactory. A voice politely suggested she should look in *Yellow Pages* or the newspapers. The British consul didn't keep a list of dog breeders but, if they could find any helpful information in their files, they would send it to her.

She sighed and paid for her call. As she was about to leave, a young man, with long hair loosely tied in a pigtail, came in. Politely he held the door open for her. Miss Beamish felt certain he was English. She half looked back and almost fell over the dog that was just outside.

'I'm awfully sorry!' exclaimed the young woman who was trying to keep the dog from following the man. If it hadn't been for the fact that she was holding on to an enormous Airedale Terrier, Miss Beamish would have given a nod and walked on. She had deliberately chosen to live away from the places where English people gathered. She wanted to be on her own.

Only the dog made her ignore the self-imposed barrier. If only it had been an Irish Setter, but

27

that was too much to expect. However, it was the nearest to what she was looking for – a needle in a haystack. So, nervously, but with almost desperate determination, Miss Beamish found herself saying, 'I wonder if you could help me?'

There was a café across the road, with white plastic tables among the orange trees that lined the pavement. Here, Miss Beamish somewhat stiffly told her story to this hippie-looking couple whose names were Jake and Merry. They were very interested in Miss Beamish's plight but, of course, they had no idea where an Irish Setter could be found.

'Does it have to be a Setter?' asked Jake, pushing strands of long wavy hair off his face. 'Wouldn't an Airedale do? Madge is about to have puppies any day now and we'll have to find homes for them.'

At the mention of her name, Madge jumped up and almost knocked the table over. Miss Beamish eyed her somewhat nervously. She was such a *big* dog!

'They're pedigree puppies and we'll register them with the Kennel Club in England if we can,' said Merry, who then rushed into telling *their* story.

Jake was an artist and Merry was a teacher of English as a foreign language. They'd lived in Spain for several years and a friend had lent them his seaside chalet for a few weeks over Christmas. It was only a kilometre from the beach, opposite the pine woods. They'd hardly settled into the chalet when Merry had to rush back to England because her father had had a heart attack. He lived on his own, except for the dog, and made her promise to take care of it. He'd thought he was going to die.

'I couldn't say no, could I?' she pleaded. 'So I had to bring her back here with me. Dad didn't tell me she was having puppies. I only found out when I got the Vet's Certificate to bring her out here. I nearly panicked then,' she laughed. 'But even though Dad recovered, he's not fit enough to look after his dog any more. So here she is.'

Jake joined in. 'The vet said there'd be a good market here for pedigree dogs so we're trying to find out. I've just been phoning someone now.'

'Poor Madge!' exclaimed Merry. 'She's so insecure at present. We're hoping she'll settle down before she gives birth. It ought to be a peaceful time, don't you think?'

Miss Beamish had to admit that she knew nothing about such things. By the end of the conversation, she had agreed that she would try to persuade Pepe to have an Airedale instead of an Irish Setter. Merry and Jake agreed that they would try to find out if a Setter could be had.

'If he wants to see the puppies, bring him along any time,' suggested Jake, and he gave Miss Beamish their address.

She felt quite pleased with herself when she went to The Beach Café the next morning. Pepe was at school but she sat with the rest of the family round her, the dog book open on the table between them. She wanted them to see what an Airedale Terrier looked like.

They did some talking among themselves, far too fast for Miss Beamish to be able to understand.

But to her relief, José finally said, 'For us okay. We like. But . . .' He shrugged by way of apology. 'First we see what Pepe say.'

'If he sees the puppies I'm sure he'll love them,' Miss Beamish urged. 'They'll be born any day now.' She couldn't imagine him being able to resist any puppy, pedigree or not, Setter or not.

José shrugged again. 'We see,' he said. 'Now we have surprise for you.'

At this Big Pepe returned to the kitchen and Maria went for plates and serviettes. With a sinking heart, Miss Beamish hoped they weren't going to bring out the favourite local delicacy – snails. Even at the risk of upsetting them, she would just have to refuse. She could see from José's expression that he expected her to enjoy whatever was coming. If only she could get away from this family and have nothing more to do with them! But it was too late . . .

Big Pepe came back with a large plate balanced on his right hand. He held it high and proudly, like a professional waiter. Carefully, he placed it in the centre of the table. On it, snuggled in a nest of paper serviettes, were some kind of cakes or biscuits, each one curled upwards like a half-open shell. They were a pale creamy colour, the crinkled edges slightly browned. Miss Beamish couldn't help smiling her relief.

'You try,' said José.

All three eagerly watched as she bit into one, delight shining in their faces at her surprise. What had looked like something hard or crisp melted like powder in her mouth into what tasted like a rush of honey. The expectant silence continued as she finished it off.

'My son. He clever. Yes?' demanded José, after insisting that Miss Beamish try a second one.

Then she understood that this delicacy was Big Pepe's own invention. She could hardly believe that he could have thought up something like this, and produced it, in the primitive kitchen of The Beach Café.

She was made to help herself to a third before they dealt with the rest. In a few moments, all that remained was the ruffled nest and a couple of crumbs. Miss Beamish began to wonder if she'd dreamt their taste and texture.

How did Big Pepe make them? That was his secret which he shared with no one. Stuck for hours in the kitchen because he wasn't very good at making friends, he painstakingly tried out all sorts of ideas.

'What do you call them? *Como tu llamar*?' Miss Beamish asked him, wondering how he could be so clever, and so wasted, at The Beach Café.

Big Pepe hadn't thought of a name. His serious face went extra serious for a moment. Then he smiled shyly and told her in Spanish, '*Alas de Angel*,' (Angels' Wings).

By the time she left them, Miss Beamish had forgotten that she'd wished she'd never become involved with this family. She went home quite pleased that she'd fulfilled her quest. However, when she came again to find out what Pepe had to say about the Airedale, her hopes were dashed.

'I have Setter,' he told her firmly. (He pronounced it Sett-air.)

'But there is no Setter,' explained Miss Beamish, feeling very frustrated. 'There is Airedale but no Setter.'

'I have Setter,' Pepe said once more.

Miss Beamish wanted to ask him how he could be so certain, but she gave up, realising that nothing would make him change his mind. 'No dog for Christmas then,' she said instead, feeling almost pleased about disappointing him.

Pepe just grinned and hugged his book. (She'd been showing him the picture of the Airedale.)

'I have,' he said. 'You see.'

Chapter five

José didn't really understand just how much Pepe wanted an Irish Setter. The biggest desire of his heart was for his son to have what he wanted – a special dog, a pedigree dog. But, to him, a dog was a dog. He was eager to settle for an Airedale Terrier. 'The bird in the hand', he called it.

The whole family argued about it. José reminded Pepe that at first he wanted a Lassie dog. 'A Setter isn't a Lassie dog.'

'It's got long hair as well,' Big Pepe replied in his brother's defence.

'Long hair, short hair? What does it matter?' asked José.

'I think short hair is better,' Maria voted. 'Dogs have fleas. The longer the hair, the more fleas he'll have.'

'How do you know?' demanded Pepe. 'And, anyway, we can buy flea powder and kill them all.'

'You'll need twice as much for a hairy dog so it's double the cost.'

Pepe knew how careful they had to be about money. It was often in their prayers. The Lord always provided but he didn't want them to be wasteful.

'I won't let him get fleas,' he retorted confidently. 'I'll bath him every day. He'll be the cleanest dog in the world.'

'It's not a question of fleas. It's a question of possibilities.' This was José again. His hard life had taught him to be very practical about things. 'When something is put in your hand, you don't just turn it down. How can we say no, when the English lady has worked so hard for us?'

'Perhaps this is the way God is answering your prayer,' suggested Big Pepe. 'Perhaps for God one sort of dog is as good as another.'

Pepe struggled with this idea. He was so certain in his heart about the Setter. He had even thought of a name for it. He was going to call it 'Red' in English. He wouldn't be able to call the Airedale 'Red'.

'We might even get him for a special price,' said Maria, with her Gypsy instinct to drive a good bargain. 'Those English people need to find homes for the puppies quickly.'

Seeing how miserable he looked, she gave him a big hug. 'Once he's yours,' she said softly, 'what difference will it make if he's one thing or another? Won't you love him the same?'

'But you're always saying the Lord will answer our prayers, even though we have to wait.'

Pepe's dark eyes flashed challengingly at them all. They didn't seem to understand. It wasn't only the dog, though it filled his thoughts day and night. It was as if they were saying he couldn't be sure that Jesus would give him what he'd asked for.

'He doesn't always answer the way we expect,'

his mother said. 'You prayed for a dog. The English lady has found you a lovely dog.'

'I didn't pray for a dog. I prayed for an Irish Setter.'

'Perhaps you're just being pig-headed,' suggested Big Pepe. 'Perhaps this is a lesson for you.'

'What lesson?'

'To accept what God gives you, not just what you want.'

Pepe ended up by bursting into tears. He wanted to please his family but they were confusing him.

'My dog is going to be a miracle,' he insisted when at last he could speak. 'I want to wait.'

His father looked at his tear-stained face and pleading eyes. 'Forgive me, son,' he said. 'You're right. We have no right to take away your miracle. Perhaps you have more faith than we do.'

No more was said about the Airedale. Instead, they started making plans for Christmas. The church was going to have a party and everyone was expected to invite someone to it.

'It would be good to invite the English lady,' suggested Maria.

'And her friends, the ones with the dog,' added José. 'They've invited us to their house. We should visit them and invite them in return.'

They all agreed and decided to pray for them every night. Before going to bed they always had a time of prayer and singing. It was the part of the day that Pepe liked best.

Although Maria had lived for many years away from her own people, she liked to do things the Gypsy way whenever she could. Gypsies love bonfires, so every night on that deserted winter beach they had a big fire. They sat round it and talked about all sorts of things while waiting for their supper to cook in the pot balanced over the heat. The stars and moon shone from the vast and often cloudless sky, adding their light to the glow from the red-hot embers.

Pepe would sit with his homework on his knees, with just enough light to sort out his sums and grammar. Big Pepe often stared silently at the flames, thinking his own thoughts. After supper, José would read something from the Bible. He was a slow reader but that didn't matter. It gave them all time to take in the words and remember them. Big Pepe read too fast, so José didn't often hand the Bible over to him. They would talk about the reading and after that they would pray.

Then Maria would start singing in her Gypsy way, beginning with a sigh from the depths of her heart. Before she had known Jesus, it had been a sigh of great sorrow. Now it was a way of saying how full of joy she felt. She often made up the words as she went along and they echoed across the sea, mingling with the never ending sigh of the waves.

They would all join in, praising God for his goodness and love. Then, when the ashes were losing their warmth and the chill of the night took over, they would go to bed, shutting the door of The Beach Café, warm and full in both heart and body.

The whole family wore their best clothes when they went to Jake and Merry's house, as if they were going to the Sunday meeting. Pepe's unruly curls were pressed into some kind of order by a liberal soaking with eau-de-Cologne and for once he looked very serious. Although everyone had promised him that he didn't have to choose one of the puppies if he really didn't want one, he knew what they were all hoping. Miss Beamish would be there, too. How could he let her down?

Jake and Merry were staying in a chalet at the far edge of the town. Theirs was the only one that had lights beaming across the dark stretch of waste ground between the chalets and the road. It was the only road out of the town. Along one side of it was a plantation of tall pine trees, a favourite place for picnickers in summertime who wanted to keep out of the sun. Few people went there in winter. Miss Beamish, who loved walking, had tried it once but the ground was so littered with rusty tins, broken bottles, dirty paper and plastic bags. She didn't go there again.

It was a good evening. Jake and Merry spoke Spanish well and seemed to know how to make everyone feel at ease. In spite of her shyness, Maria was intensely curious about their lifestyle. She was astonished that their beautiful chalet could be so untidy, especially the kitchen. Neither Merry nor Jake bothered very much about washing-up or putting things away.

Jake managed to get Big Pepe talking about fishing. He showed him some sketches of fishing boats in the town's little harbour while Merry carefully introduced Pepe to Madge.

At first, Pepe was scared of Madge. She was so big and powerful and excitable, and her giant paws seemed to be everywhere at once. Even though the living room was about as big as the whole of

The Beach Café, Madge somehow made it seem small.

The puppies were in a spare bedroom, nestled in a jumble of blankets on the floor. Merry took Pepe and his father to see them while Madge was kept out of the way. Her protesting whines and barks showed that she knew what was going on and wasn't too pleased about it.

Pepe just stared in silent wonder as the clump of sleeping puppies woke up and started unwinding themselves from each other. They were blindly looking for their mother and made funny, squeaky noises. Delight spread slowly over his face. He'd never seen such baby creatures before.

Merry put one of them into his hands and he pressed it against his cheek.

'Do you like him?' she asked with a smile.

He gave a silent nod.

'You see,' said his father. 'Didn't I tell you? The bird in the hand . . .' He was feeling very pleased.

'But it's not my Setter,' Pepe replied, and all José could do was look at Merry with a shrug of apology.

Even so, it was very hard for Pepe to let go of that puppy. He had never held anything so warm and so soft and so helpless. It gave him a very special feeling. If he shut his eyes, this little creature could be his Setter. Would a Setter puppy be any more cuddly or delightful than this little thing?

He was left on his own with the puppies and he sat on the tiled floor beside their nest, caressing each one in turn, admiring their perfectly formed little bodies. They hadn't yet opened their eyes, though Merry said they'd do that at any moment, and their ears were still quite squashed against their skulls.

While he sat there, waiting to see if their eyes would open, a battle was going on inside him. Did his dog have to be a Setter? Suppose a Setter never came? How long ought he to wait for Jesus to answer his prayer? Would it be wrong to have one of these puppies? His family didn't seem to think so.

He wished he hadn't been brought to see them. The temptation to stop believing that Jesus had heard and would answer his prayer was very strong.

Just then a loud volley of barks burst from Madge. There was a hefty bang against the bedroom door as she tried to get back to her pups. She knew Pepe had been a long time on his own with them and she was getting anxious. Pepe was startled. He almost dropped the puppy he was handling and his heart beat fast.

Then he remembered how strong and tall their mother was; square and solid and pushy. She really wasn't his sort of dog, not like his Setter. His Setter would be gentle and elegant, with ears and hair that flowed like the manes of the beautiful horses that sometimes galloped along the beach.

Madge's hair was as hard as a brush – a bit like his brother's had been when he had to do his army service and came home with his hair cropped short. Everybody had laughed and Pepe remembered how bristly Big Pepe's head had felt.

These puppies were soft now but, one day, they'd be stiff and soldierly like their mother. They were not for him. And he was able to put the last one back with its brothers without any regrets. The yearning had stopped. The confusion was gone.

He jumped up and rejoined his family. His heart was again at peace.

José invited all the English people to the church Christmas celebration and they agreed to go, even Miss Beamish. She had never enjoyed Christmas. She'd never had anyone to celebrate it with. It was only because they were all laughing together, and because she felt she owed something to them for being kind to her, that she agreed to go.

Whatever the reasons they all had for saying yes, Pepe's parents could only see everything as an answer to their prayers. They went home praising God without even remembering to ask Pepe what he had decided.

Chapter six

The church met at the house of the blue-haired lady. It was an old Andalusian house with iron grilles at the small windows and thick walls to keep out the sun and heat. It had a large patio, full of plants and flowers and canaries in cages.

Sister Dolores had set one room aside for meetings. Normally there were about twelve grown-ups and a similar number of children. But because it was a special occasion, both the room and patio bustled with people and noise. Tables had been set up, draped with white cloths. As people came, the tables gradually filled with food – fish, chicken, eggs, potato salads, cold meats of every kind, olives, cheese, mountains of crisps, bottles of orange, lemon and wine, and different kinds of cakes and marzipans.

It was the sort of meeting the children liked best. When they weren't running about the patio, they had their eyes on all that was on the tables, longing for the moment when thanks would be given to God and they could all start eating. Big Pepe had prepared an enormous dish of Angels' Wings which, at present, were hidden under a white cloth. Outside the family, no one but Miss Beamish had ever tasted them.

As for Miss Beamish, she was quite surprised. So were Jake and Merry. They had expected to find themselves in the old church in the main square, not in someone's home. Jake said this to one of the men there, who explained that this was how the first believers used to meet. He opened his Bible and read out what it said about the believers meeting in each other's homes.

'We share together as they did,' he said. 'We pray for each other. We help each other when we can, and God is good to us.'

Jake translated all this for Miss Beamish who was looking a bit uncomfortable. Miss Beamish had been brought up in an orphanage and made to go to church three times every Sunday. She still remembered the hard pews, the sermons that went on for ever, the hymns she couldn't understand, and the cold. She could only ever remember being cold in church.

The way these people worshipped God astonished her. The singing was so noisy! Everyone clapped their hands or played castanets, and the children didn't have to sit still but ran about as they pleased. Was it just because it was Christmas? Miss Beamish hadn't been to church since those long ago days. She began to wonder what she might have thought about God if she'd been allowed to enjoy herself as everyone about her was doing.

Jake translated some of what the preacher was saying. It was the usual Christmas story which she had resented so much as a child. She had been abandoned by her parents without ever knowing who they were. That baby, born in a manger, had been better off than herself. Someone had loved him. No one had ever loved her.

She pressed her lips together, even as she let that old resentment press painfully in her heart again. She had once prayed and prayed that her unknown mother would come to the orphanage and take her home. Then she had prayed and prayed that any kind woman would take her home and love her. It never happened, so she stopped believing in God.

'God loves you,' the preacher was saying. She could understand enough Spanish for that. '*Dios te ama*', he said again, and it seemed as if . . . as if – ridiculous thought – that God knew what was in her heart that very moment.

'Nonsense,' she told herself, but those three words refused to go away.

Two other things happened at that Christmas party. One of the strangers there was Sister Dolores's nephew. He owned a high-class bakery and cafeteria in Madrid. He insisted that Big Pepe's Angels' Wings were the most incredible thing he had ever tasted. He wanted Big Pepe to go to Madrid and make Angels' Wings for him all day long.

'I can make you rich,' he told him. 'We'll make each other rich. You'll be famous.'

Maria overheard this. She didn't like the idea of Big Pepe going so far from home, and to a big city where anything might happen to him.

'He doesn't need money or fame,' she told the

43

nephew. 'Don't tempt him. He's better off here with us.'

She dragged him away, but not before the man had given Big Pepe a card with his name and address. Big Pepe put it in his pocket, though he said nothing, but every now and then he felt to make sure it was still there.

One of the church members was the telephonist and she told José she had a message for him. The building contractor he often worked for had phoned. There was work on a building site in the north for three or four months. If he was interested he must phone as soon as possible.

'Praise God!' exclaimed José. 'Did he say if there was work for my son, too?' It was his dream to take Big Pepe with him so that he could start earning a living. But there was only work for him. They only wanted people with experience.

'It's not fair!' he exclaimed to the family. 'How can he get experience if he never has a job?'

'I have been offered a job,' Big Pepe reminded them. 'That man from Madrid. He says any time I want, I can work for him. He wanted the recipe for my Angels' Wings. He even offered to pay me for it but I wouldn't let him have it.'

There was silence. Pepe knew that no one wanted his brother to go so far away from home. It was bad enough when their father had to be away for several months. But at least they knew he would be coming back. If Big Pepe went to Madrid, would he ever come back to stay?

'It's my big chance,' Big Pepe insisted. 'Something I really want to do.'

'Wait till I come back,' said José. 'We'll talk and pray about it then.'

'Then you'll want me to stay for the summer. And perhaps the man will have changed his mind.' There was a hint of resentment in his voice.

'If he has, then no problem,' shrugged his father. 'We'll pray about it when I come back. But don't leave your mother and brother alone while I'm away.'

Big Pepe said no more but Pepe could see that he was still thinking about it. They shared a mattress which was put down on the café floor at the end of each day. That night, Pepe said to him, 'I don't want you to go away. It'll be worse than when you were in the army. You used to come home most weekends.'

'I'd come home for holidays. And you could come and stay with me sometimes, too.'

'What will it be like there? Will I be able to take my dog with me?'

Big Pepe laughed. 'You still haven't got a dog. And when you do have him, you won't miss me.'

'But why do you want to go?' insisted Pepe.

'I want to do something with my life. You'll understand when you get to my age.'

'Is twenty very old?' wondered Pepe. He'd never thought much about his brother being grown up and it made him feel sad. 'I wish you were only my age.'

'Go to sleep,' was Big Pepe's reply.

Pepe shut his eyes but he couldn't sleep. There was too much to think about. The whole town was getting ready for 'Kings'. At school the rumour had gone round that someone would be riding a camel in the procession, but that was hard to believe. Pepe had never seen a real camel. And the shop windows were full of toys. Most of the boys wanted bikes that year. They boasted and argued about which was best and which they might get and that made Pepe think about his dog again.

Would he get something else if he couldn't have a dog? What did he want? No one had asked him. They must be planning a surprise.

At last the great day came. When Pepe woke up he found that overnight a row of little packages had been laid out on the counter for him. Everyone watched while he excitedly tore off the wrappings. There was a calendar with six different photos of dogs, including an Irish Setter; four tins of dog food; a packet of dog rice; a tub of flea powder; a brush and comb and – best of all – a green collar and lead.

Pepe sniffed the new leather. It had a very special smell.

'All that's lacking is the dog,' laughed his brother.

'Not for long,' boasted Pepe, stroking the leather and sniffing it again.

'I'll get you a dog in the north,' promised his father. 'When I come back I'll bring one with me. You'll see.'

'But only an Irish Setter,' warned Pepe.

'Whatever you say,' said José.

Miss Beamish came along later with a present. It was a book on how to look after pet dogs and they looked at it together. Big Pepe had been up early to make Angels' Wings. They were his present to the English lady for trying to help them with the dog.

They all went together to watch the procession which set out from the main square at midday. Merry and Jake were there, taking lots of photos. They'd left Madge at home with the puppies. But just then Pepe wasn't thinking about dogs. Like all the children, his mind was on collecting as many sweets as possible. They were scattered like rain in generous handfuls by the people on the floats who were dressed very fancifully as the Kings' attendants. There was plenty of scrabbling, pushing and quarrelling, especially when footballs were being tossed down. It wasn't fair when the parents grabbed them for their children!

There was a camel but it wasn't a real one. It was a costume with two people inside it. It blundered all over the place, its 'boy' stuffing its mouth with all the sweets he could steal from the children. It frightened the horses and made them rear, but the camel itself got a fright when someone tied firecrackers to its tail.

Everyone enjoyed themselves, though quite a few people ended up with toothache, including Pepe.

The next morning, all the family walked with José to the bus-stop. He had a very long journey ahead of him which would take him two days on different buses and coaches. It was always sad when he went away but, as usual, he promised to phone them at the Telephone Exchange every week. He wasn't any good at writing letters.

Pepe took the collar and lead with him. He

wanted to practise walking his dog. It wasn't hard to pretend that Red was on the other end.

'Just you wait and see what a beautiful dog I'm going to bring you,' were his father's last words to him as he gave him an extra hug before getting on the bus.

They stood waving him goodbye until the bus was out of sight, whether or not he could see them. What none of them knew just then was that a time of great sorrow and testing was coming very soon to them all.

Chapter seven

One day, Miss Beamish was surprised to find Jake calling at her door.

'You're not going to believe this,' he began with a grin, 'but I think I've found an Irish Setter.'

'Well I never!' was all Miss Beamish could say for the moment. Then, in a rush, 'Where? How did you hear about it? How much is it going to cost?'

'Hang on! Hang on!' exclaimed Jake. 'Wait till you've heard the story.'

Mystified, she invited Jake in. It was the first time she'd had a visitor in her little house but she was too astonished by Jake's news to be flustered.

Pushing his long wavy hair from his face, Jake began, 'You know the pine woods opposite the chalets? We sometimes take Madge for a walk over there. Not very often. It's a bit of a mess—'

'You needn't tell me,' agreed Miss Beamish primly. 'I tried it once.'

'Anyway, we were there yesterday and found this dog. Or, rather, it found us. You wouldn't believe the state it's in. I don't know how long it's been there. I reckon someone must have dumped it from a car, perhaps some time ago.'

'A pedigree dog?' wondered Miss Beamish. 'A Setter?'

'Well, we think it is. A young one, perhaps not a year old yet. It's a bit difficult to tell. It's lost half its hair. It's got some horrible skin complaint. That could be because it's half-starved. It looks awful.'

'Where is it now?'

'At home, in the patio. I wanted to leave it where it was. I didn't want Madge or the pups to catch anything. But Merry said, no way. She brought it home. It's a pathetic thing; so grateful, just for a kind word. We're feeding her on vitamin tablets, raw liver, milk and cereal. The question is: do we have her put down or do we ask Pepe if he wants her?'

'How sure are you that it's a Setter?'

Jake hesitated. ' . . . Let's say sixty percent. It could be some sort of retriever, I suppose. I'm not an expert.'

'Pepe would know. But if it's in such a bad way, would it be fair to let him see it?'

'Merry reckons that if she were Pepe and this were her only chance of getting the dog she wanted, she'd take it, whatever the problems.'

'Perhaps she's right,' said Miss Beamish thoughtfully. 'How can we decide for him? But come with me to explain. My Spanish isn't good enough.'

Pepe was at school so Jake told his story again to Maria and Big Pepe. 'It's a very sick dog,' he insisted. 'If you don't want Pepe to know about it, I'll understand.'

'If it's a Setter then it must be his dog,' said Maria, and she explained how Pepe had prayed for this miracle. 'Surely you can see it's a miracle?' she demanded, her black eyes gleaming.

'Well, I don't know about that,' answered Jake. 'I'm not really into religion . . .'

He turned to Miss Beamish and explained with a grin, 'She says it's the dog Pepe's been waiting for. Apparently, he's been expecting a miracle and God has performed one.'

'It is very odd,' remarked Miss Beamish, and wondered why she felt so uncomfortable. She wanted to scoff, but she couldn't.

When Pepe saw his mother and brother at the school gate that afternoon he knew something special must be happening.

'Well, you've got your answer!' Big Pepe exclaimed, pretending to punch his ear. 'Hurry. We're going to the English people's house.'

'What's happening? Is it my dog? It is, isn't it? I've got my dog. He's come! He's come!'

They hardly had time to tell him that he was going to see a sick dog. Maria began to explain how Jake had found it, but she spent more time praising God for answered prayer. Pepe was hardly listening anyway and ran ahead. They were too slow for him.

His face was flushed and his eyes were bright as Merry opened the door.

'Where's my dog?' The words burst out of him as he looked eagerly from side to side, expecting it to come lolloping up to him, or to be in someone's arms, ready to be handed over.

'You'll see her in a minute,' said Jake. 'But we need to talk about her first.'

51

'It's a girl!' exclaimed Pepe. He'd never thought of his Red being a girl.

'She's very sick—' began Jake, but Pepe interrupted him.

'It doesn't matter. I'll look after her. I'll make her better. Where is she? I want to see her.'

The dog was curled up on some newspapers in a corner of the patio. Jake let Pepe go out on his own to her, only warning, 'Don't touch her. She's in a bit of a mess. And be very quiet and gentle. Don't startle her.'

He needn't have worried. Pepe was suddenly overawed by the moment he'd longed for. There was his Red, the dog Jesus knew all about and had sent to him.

'Red,' he almost whispered.

As the dog went on sleeping he said the name again, just a little bit louder. This time the sticky eyelids opened and she looked at him. Although it was a sickly gaze, Pepe's heart pounded with excitement. How often had that same gaze met him from the page in his book?

With a confident grin, he stretched out a hand, snapping his fingers. 'Red!' he exclaimed. 'Don't you know me? I'm Pepe, your friend.'

To his delight, the hairless tail gave a little twitch. Pepe laughed.

'You're so ugly!' he exclaimed. 'But I love you just the same. I'll make you the most beautiful dog in the world.'

The tail gave two more feeble twitches.

'Do you think you're going to love me?' Pepe asked her. 'I hope so, because you belong to me.

I asked Jesus for you, especially, and here you are.'

The dog made an effort to get up but fell back with a whimper.

'It's no good feeling sorry for yourself,' Pepe told her. 'You've got to get better. You've got to get strong. Come on. Try again.'

He clicked his fingers and grinned as she heaved herself up, a patchy, swaying scarecrow, tail wagging in weak apology. He forgot that Jake had told him not to touch her. He took a couple of paces towards her and knelt down, putting out his hand to smooth over her head and ears. Those bits had hair, anyway.

She wasn't soft and silky, like the dog in his book. There was dirt, fleas and sores all over her, and she trembled at Pepe's touch. She licked his fingers nervously, hardly able to believe that there was a human hand to caress her once more.

'Red,' said Pepe. It was a love word, and he said it again, 'Red. That's your name. It's English. Do you like it? I think it's all right for a girl. I'm going to take you home and make you better. When my father comes back you'll be so beautiful, he just won't believe it.'

That night, Red was sharing Pepe's supper on the beach. The flickering firelight and the dark were kind to her. Her pitiful condition could hardly be seen. Maria had bought some herbs and lard and they were melting together in a pot.

'We Gypsies know a thing or two about cures. She'll soon have her hair again,' she promised.

'But we'll still give her the pills, won't we?' said

Pepe. Jake had given him the vitamins and liver, along with advice about careful feeding.

'Pills, ointment, love and prayer,' laughed Maria. 'How can she not get well and beautiful with all that?'

'And I can tell Papa all about her on Saturday, can't I?' demanded Pepe. 'He needs to know, in case he brings another Setter, like he said.'

When he worked away from home, José always phoned every Saturday afternoon. The family would go along to the Telephone Exchange and wait for the call to come through. It was always an exciting event, but this time it would be extra special.

Big Pepe did the Bible reading now and he read the story of the lost sheep.

'Suppose one of you has a hundred sheep and loses one of them – what does he do? He leaves the other ninety-nine sheep in the pasture and goes looking for the one that got lost until he finds it. When he finds it, he is so happy that he puts it on his shoulders and carries it back home. Then he calls his friends and neighbours together and says to them, "I am so happy I found my lost sheep. Let us celebrate!" '

Pepe thought of how his brother had carried Red home in his arms and he sighed with contentment.

'Red was like a lost sheep,' he said, 'and Jesus knew where she was. And I'm like the shepherd, aren't I, even though I didn't exactly find her myself? Jesus would have helped me find her if the English people hadn't found her first, wouldn't he?'

54

'It's a miracle,' agreed his mother. 'And if Jesus cares so much about lost sheep and lost dogs, how much more does he care about lost people?'

Before they went to bed they prayed for all the people in the town who were lost because they didn't know Jesus as their Lord and Saviour.

Pepe couldn't sleep that night. His mother wouldn't allow Red indoors and he kept wondering how she was, all on her own. When he thought Big Pepe was asleep, he sneaked out to check. She was curled up in a tight ball, almost on top of the ashes which was all that was left of the bonfire.

It was cold. He sat down beside her and hugged his arms round his chest to keep warm. Gratefully, she crept closer to him. Soon he felt her dry black muzzle pushing its way under his elbow and nudging his ribs. Just then he was the happiest boy in the world!

Big Pepe came and sat quietly beside him. After a while he said, 'You're going to be really daft with that dog!' But he said it in a friendly way.

'Does that dog book of yours say if Irish Setters are good guard dogs?' he asked after a long silence.

'Why?'

'Because I've decided I'm going away and you and Red can look after Mama until our father comes back.'

Pepe was stunned. 'But . . . but . . . Papa said to wait till he comes home. How can you go without his permission?'

'Because I'm twenty years old and for the first time in my life I have a chance to do something I really want to do, something I know I'll be good at.'

'But why don't you do it here?'

'Because here nobody wants what I can do. How many Angels' Wings are the people here going to eat? There are five million people in Madrid.'

'Five million! How can you make so many Angels' Wings? You won't have time to sleep.'

'Don't be silly,' Big Pepe laughed. 'And don't say anything to Mama until I've told her myself. I just want you to be on my side when I do tell her.'

'But I don't want you to go either.'

'You've got Red now. You don't need me.'

Chapter eight

Pepe's first days with Red were a far cry from what he had imagined – the cuddly puppy he could carry everywhere or the playful companion dancing along the seashore at his side. As for jumping through hoops and opening doors . . . He had to be content with sitting beside her, stroking her head and picking out fleas and ticks. All she wanted to do was sleep and eat and sleep again.

He couldn't even cuddle her because of the foul ointment his mother had brewed and then smothered her with. It stank, so that even sitting beside her wasn't exactly pleasant.

To encourage both Red and himself, Pepe would get out his dog book and show her his favourite photo.

'That's you,' he told her. 'Take a good look. That's what you'll be like when you're better.'

She licked the page with her tongue, but Pepe wasn't sure if it was because she wanted to eat it or because she recognised herself. All she thought about was food. Her appetite was enormous. Miss Beamish brought a bag of liver and a carton of milk every now and then, as well as more vitamin pills, and Red also shared whatever came out of the cooking pot each night.

Pepe was patient. Every day he prayed for Red and every day she grew stronger. It had taken him days to comb through the tangled mess of the hair that remained on her head and legs, being careful not to hurt or frighten her. Then came the exciting day when her skin started to look whole and clean and there were signs of fluffy, copper-coloured hair coming through.

In the beginning she'd had no strength for walks or games. All Pepe could do with the green leather collar and lead was show them to her and tell her of all the places they would go to together one day. But as the bald patches began to disappear and a shine slowly came to her coat, her playful character began to show itself too. The lanky legs moved less stiffly and began to prance. Her once pus-caked eyes were clean again, and there was a gleam that put joy in Pepe's heart.

Everyone could now tell that she was an Irish Setter and that she was going to be beautiful.

'I think love and care have done as much for that dog as vitamins,' Miss Beamish said to Jake and Merry when they came along with her one day to see how Pepe was getting on with Red.

'And prayer,' added Pepe when Jake told him what she'd said. 'When I'm sick, Jesus always makes me better.'

Jake and Merry were going away the next day with Madge and all the puppies. Merry's pupils were waiting for her. Jake had done a quick pencil sketch of Madge curled up with her puppies in the blankets. He'd also done a more detailed sketch of Red.

'A goodbye present,' he told Pepe, whose eyes shone with surprised joy.

Big Pepe made his special Angels' Wings for them. They sat round one of the outside tables in the warm winter sun. Everyone chatted in a mixture of English and Spanish. Merry took some snapshots and promised to send copies to Miss Beamish for everybody. 'Perhaps we'll come back one day,' she said.

Miss Beamish was surprised to realise how much she was enjoying herself. The Spanish climate was having a strange effect on her! She had never enjoyed herself like this in England.

Maria was daring enough to invite them all to the Sunday meeting. Afterwards, she felt shaky and disappeared into the kitchen, only coming out to say goodbye when they all left. Later, she said the Lord must have given her the boldness and the words because she'd never dared do such a thing before. But she knew it was the right thing because the English lady said yes – and she came.

'The Lord is softening her heart,' she said. 'Perhaps by the time your father comes home she'll be one of us.'

Once Red got her strength back, she wanted to follow Pepe everywhere. This was great, except when he had to go to school. Then he had to use the collar and lead for tying her up. It was no use just shutting her in the house. The minute the door was open she'd be off, looking for him.

Pepe's heart swelled with pride at her devotion. Now Red was his dog, not just because she'd been brought to him, but because she wanted to be with him. She was friendly with his mother and brother but her gaze was always on him. Whatever he was doing, she'd be watching him. Even when she was asleep, every now and then she'd open her eyes to make sure he was there.

More and more she looked just like the dog in his book, her ears long and silky, her movements as free and proud as the dancing horses of the region. If only Papa could see her! If only she'd come to him before he'd gone away!

They raced along the beach together – Red always won. They struggled up the sand-hills, Pepe sometimes reaching the top first. They paddled at the water's edge because it was too cold for swimming. Would she be a good swimmer? She tried biting the water that tickled her paws and decided she didn't like it very much. Pepe laughed at her comical surprise. They had their own one-a-side football team, Red usually hogging the ball. She wasn't much good at scoring goals so Pepe's side – Betis – was the best.

They did everything together except at bedtime. Then Red had to be tied up outside and Pepe had to try not to hear her whimperings and scratchings.

'I don't know why she can't share our bed,' Pepe grumbled to his brother, one night. 'She's clean now. She hasn't any fleas and the scabs are all gone.'

'Be patient,' Big Pepe replied. 'You'll soon have the bed all to yourself. Then you can do what you like with it.'

That shut Pepe up.

The very next night, while they were having supper, Big Pepe dropped his bombshell. He would be going to Madrid in eight days' time. It was a quiet bombshell because Big Pepe was a quiet sort of person, but it was devastating.

Pepe had never seen his mother so upset and angry. But whatever she said and however much she pleaded, Big Pepe's mind was made up and his plans were laid. When he wouldn't give way, she began to moan that something bad would happen if he went away before his father came home.

'What's going to happen? Tell me. You're just trying to scare me into staying,' Big Pepe eventually exploded.

'I can feel it. Like a darkness in my heart. You can't feel it but I can.'

'That's just Gypsy talk,' he replied angrily.

Pepe wanted to shrink into the darkness beyond the fire's glow. His whole body was hot, but it was from the pain of what was happening, not from the burning wood. Even Red was disturbed. She pressed hard against him and began to whine. She was afraid of human anger.

'You're upsetting my dog,' he cried in her defence, putting his arms round her. 'Why don't you both stop?'

Surprised by his pain, they did. But a deep shadow had fallen over them all. Not even the dancing flames, which Big Pepe had angrily stirred up a few minutes before, could melt the hardness that seemed to have entered their hearts.

After a long silence Maria said, 'Read something from the Bible.'

Big Pepe obeyed but they could tell that his heart was not in the words. Somehow, they didn't sound the same.

The next few days were very hard. Pepe had never known such unhappiness at home. It was one thing to have an argument. Every family had those. But this was two of the people he loved most set against each other. And Papa wasn't there to sort it out.

He was glad to have Red to sneak away with. As soon as he came home from school he was off with her. While he had bread and chocolate in his hands she stayed close, begging her share with doleful eyes and wagging tail, licking her jaws in expectation. Then she would gallop off like a bullet, glad to be free, glad to be with Pepe. Usually, he'd run his fastest after her, making it a race which she always won.

But now he didn't feel like running. He felt more like crying, and she kept stopping to look back at him, as if to ask him why he was so slow. She was so beautiful when she looked at him like that, ears held high, one paw lifted, the wind playing through her hair.

He wandered one evening with troubled heart along the edge of the sea, the cloud-laden sky darkening rapidly. He wondered if Big Pepe still would have decided to go if he hadn't had Red. He hardly wanted to turn back home.

The first flames of the fire were leaping up and he could see Big Pepe throwing on a couple of planks. There was something angry in the way he did it.

Pepe's own heart was suddenly hot with anger,

too. He was angry with his brother for wanting to go and angry with his mother for not wanting to let him. He stood kicking the wet sand, letting the tears slide down his cheeks. He was too angry even to pray. He had even forgotten Red just then, until she came back to him and licked his fingers with her soft tongue.

It was like a kiss. That made him smile.

Miss Beamish knew something was wrong. There was a sullenness about Big Pepe which he could hardly hide when he brought out her mint tea, while Maria hid herself away in the kitchen.

The church family didn't know what to say. They were such a small family that it would be almost as hard for them to say goodbye to Big Pepe. Sister Dolores said her nephew in Madrid was a good man and wouldn't cheat him. When the pastor couldn't persuade Big Pepe to wait till his father came home, he told Maria to trust God and to let him go with her blessing. They all prayed about it and said they would have a special goodbye meal for his last Sunday with them.

The joy of the Saturday afternoon trip to the Telephone Exchange had turned to dread. Maria wanted José to tell his son to stay at home. Big Pepe declared that, whatever his father said, he was going. Maria spoke first, pouring out all her fears. Then it was Big Pepe's turn. He listened more than he spoke, but Pepe could see his face growing more and more stubborn. Then Maria had a second turn and spent most of it crying.

Pepe was very glad he'd been able to have a long talk about Red the week before. This Saturday there was no time left for him to say more than, 'Hello,' and hear his father reply, 'Look after your mother,' before the line went dead.

'If only you'd wait till your father comes home,' moaned Maria again as they trooped almost silently home.

'He understands, Mama. He says it's all right. You heard him. And we're going to meet in Madrid on his way home. He'll see where I am and that everything's okay. He'll tell you all about it. And I'll phone you every week, too, just like Papa.'

On the Sunday, everyone prayed for Big Pepe in a special way. Pepe began to cry because now it was certain that his brother was leaving, in spite of all his mother's tears.

Miss Beamish came to this meeting, too, and was surprised to find how sad she felt. The Beach Café family had become special to her in a way that nobody had ever been special before. She found herself really wanting there to be a God who would look after Big Pepe in the big city.

While everyone else was praying for him, standing round him in a circle of love, she found herself thinking about their God. 'I don't know who you are,' she thought, 'but if you do exist, please answer their prayers.'

She was surprised at herself. When she was only ten years old, she'd told God she would never ask him for anything again. She could still remember the bitterness of that defiant prayer. It all surged back as if it were only yesterday. But she couldn't bring herself to say sorry to God for having once talked to him like that, even though she wanted to. In fact, she decided she'd better not come to any more meetings. This funny little church was having a strange effect on her.

Pepe was allowed to have the morning off school to say goodbye to his brother at the bus-stop. Nearly everyone from the church was there, too, and Miss Beamish. Pepe took Red with him. No one from the church had seen her before and they were amazed that Pepe should have such a beautiful pedigree dog. Although he had already told them about his prayer, and the way God had answered it, they had forgotten because dogs are not very important in Spain.

When the bus came at last, the driver had to wait while everyone gave Big Pepe a hug and a kiss and some last words of advice. Miss Beamish just shook his hand. She was no good at hugs and kisses. And then he was gone, just like his father before him. The only difference was that soon his father would be back, but no one knew when they'd see Big Pepe again.

Chapter nine

'How long is it now before Papa comes home?' Pepe asked his mother after the bus had gone.

'At least two months.'

'And how long is that?'

Time had never meant very much to Pepe before now because every day had been more or less the same.

'He'll come before Easter. If it rains at the proper time, he'll come before the rain.'

'That's still a long time,' sighed Pepe.

'Yes,' agreed his mother.

'But at least Red will be as clever as Lassie by then. I'm going to start training her as soon as we get home.'

'No, you're not. You're going back to school.'

'Oh, Mama . . . We don't do anything at school this afternoon. Honest. It's just drawing and things. Please.'

Just that once she gave in and Pepe decided that the first thing he must do was make a hoop for Red to jump through. Until she had a hoop she could never learn the trick.

There was nothing useful among the jumble of odds and ends at the back of the café so, taking

Red with him, he made for the building site at the far end of the town. A big hotel was being built on the beach and there were all kinds of interesting things among the rubble. A workman saw him and asked what he was up to, so Pepe explained.

'For this dog, eh?' asked the workman with a grin. 'He's a fine-looking animal. How can a boy like you afford a dog like that?'

Pepe told the whole story again and the workman was a bit taken aback. 'So your God produces pedigree dogs out of a hat?' he joked.

'Not out of a hat,' Pepe patiently replied. 'She was in the pine woods. I told you. Somebody must have left her there.'

'Let's hope they don't come back then. You might have to give her up.'

This thought had never occurred to Pepe, or to anyone else. Could Red be lost rather than abandoned? Would anyone come looking for her? Fear clutched Pepe's heart for a moment. Then he remembered.

'No, they won't,' he boldly replied. 'My God would never give me anything that belonged to someone else.'

The man burst out laughing. 'Well said!' he exclaimed. 'Where can I find this God of yours? I need someone like him to sort out my problems.'

Pepe didn't know whether he was joking or not but he told him where the church met. 'And now, are you going to give me something to make a hoop for my dog?' he demanded.

Just then, Red bounded away from him with a bark of excitement. A rat had poked its head above a pile of rubble. What a chase there was! Pepe stood open-mouthed with astonishment and pride at the way Red zigzagged and bounded after it, her paws hardly touching the ground.

Two other dogs on the site joined in the chase with barks of excitement and the workmen put down their tools to watch, arguing over which dog would catch the rat or if it would get away. Red was terrified when the other dogs joined in. Perhaps she thought they were chasing her. She dashed back to Pepe, tail between her legs, ears flat, eyes panic-stricken.

Pepe knelt down and put his arms round her. She was quivering with fear. 'You're all right,' he soothed her. 'They're not going to hurt you. You're safe with me.'

The workmen started making jokes about her – a hunting dog that gave up on the chase!

'She's only young,' Pepe defended her. 'And she's been ill. She's only just getting better.'

The rat's life ended with a sharp squeak; the dust settled as the dogs panted triumphantly over their prey; the workman gathered round this unusual and beautiful dog that had started the chase. She flattened herself against Pepe, afraid of their rough voices.

But they were kind. Half an hour later, Pepe was dragging home a thick rusty cable which they had knocked into a hoop shape for him. They had wanted him to make Red jump through it there and then, but Pepe patiently explained that she hadn't yet learnt. He didn't care how much they teased him. He'd got what he wanted.

Red raced along the sand ahead of him, crazily happy now that the building site and the dogs were behind them. She chased the waves that tickled her paws, snapping at the foam and sneezing at its saltiness. She tossed chunks of seaweed in the air as she loped along, making Pepe laugh. She fought a growly battle with a bit of driftwood which, once defeated, she carried home to chew at leisure.

There was a clown in Red that was showing itself more and more as her health returned. She was the best dog in the world for a boy like Pepe. His laughter and her excited barks echoed across the empty beach as they made their way home.

That night, Maria made up the fire. Pepe and Red had helped by looking for fuel, but it was strange not to have Big Pepe with them. There was still the bad memory of the last week, when there'd been no reading, no singing and no prayers, not even on Big Pepe's very last night with them. Perhaps there had been secret prayers but nothing had been spoken aloud.

Both Pepe and his mother felt lonely and sad that night. Was Big Pepe remembering them as he sat on that coach on his way to Madrid? Was he too excited about his new life to be sad?

Pepe wondered if things would ever get right between Big Pepe and Mama. They still hadn't been when he went away. It was very hard to understand grown-ups and it was strange to think of Big Pepe as a grown-up, instead of just as his brother. How good it was to have Red. She'd never go away!

His mother broke into his thoughts. 'You'll have to read the Bible now,' she said, 'until your father comes home.'

Pepe didn't know what to say. The very idea scared him. How could he take his father's place? How would he know where to read?

'Don't worry,' his mother encouraged him. 'Just open it somewhere and read. All of God's word is good.'

The family Bible was a precious book which José kept wrapped in a cloth. It was big and heavy, with large letters. There were lots of things in it he didn't understand. Not knowing if he was scared or thrilled, Pepe took it from his mother and opened it, more or less in the middle.

The flickering firelight made shadows dance over the pages and it was a while before he could fix his eyes on something in particular. Then, with a shaky voice that grew firmer as he went on, he began to read:

'Do not be afraid – I am with you! I am your God – let nothing terrify you! I will make you strong and help you; I will protect you and save you.

'I am the Lord your God; I strengthen you and say, "Do not be afraid; I will help you!"'

His mother broke in at that point. 'Trouble is coming. I just know it is. And the Lord wants us to be ready for it. He's warning us in advance.'

'What kind of trouble, Mama? What's going to happen?'

All the anguish of the last few days flooded Pepe's heart again. Even though God promised to help them, he couldn't help feeling afraid.

His mother didn't know. All she said was, 'Read the words again.'

It wasn't easy to see them with tears blinking in

his eyes. It wasn't easy to say them with a lump in his throat. But somehow he got through them.

'I wish Papa would come home,' he said when he'd finished. 'He told me to look after you until he does. Red and I will do it together. And Jesus.'

While his mother was hugging him, he said, 'Mama, can Red sleep with me tonight? My brother said she could once he was gone. She doesn't have fleas now. She's clean. Please say she can.'

Maria sighed. She had been about to say that he could sleep with her, as he used to sometimes when his father was away. But she could see how much he wanted to sleep with the dog.

'All right,' she said.

He flung his arms round her. 'You're the best mother in the world,' he said. 'I'm going to love you for ever.'

It took a while to get Red settled in bed. She wanted to play, and that included a tug-of-war with the blanket and lots of yelpy growls. It was too dark for Pepe to see her properly, to get hold of her and calm her down, and his groping hands only made her more excited.

'Be quiet or my mother will throw you out,' he warned her. 'Sssh!' But he spoilt it by giggling so she didn't believe him.

At some point they both fell asleep in a very untidy jumble of bedding.

Chapter ten

Trouble came just a few days later. Pepe came flying home from school, not wanting to miss a minute with Red, only to find her not interested in playing games. Usually she came bouncing to meet him. But this afternoon, though she wagged her tail, she didn't get up. Chin on paws, she gave him a mournful look. Her nose was dry, her body was hot.

'What can it be?' he cried to his mother.

A dreadful fear was growing in his heart. Somehow he knew Red wasn't just a little bit poorly, but very poorly indeed. There was a look of fear in her eyes. She knew it too.

As the hours passed she grew worse. Maria tried all sorts of Gypsy remedies to stop the sickness. In the end, all Pepe could do was hold her in his arms and cry and pray over her.

'Please, Jesus, don't let her die. Don't let her die. Now you've just given her to me you can't let her die.'

It was the longest night Pepe had ever known. He fell asleep with his arms around her and his mother covered them both with a blanket. She hadn't the heart to separate them. She herself spent the night keeping the fire going, watching over them both and praying.

The next morning Red was still alive. Maria hurried to the Telephone Exchange and asked the telephonist to call the nearest vet. 'Tell him it's urgent. He's got to come. I don't care how much it costs. He's got to save my son's dog.'

Then she hurried back home and the morning seemed even longer while they waited for the vet to come. Red lay under the blanket, eyes closed, and Pepe sat huddled in another blanket beside her, pale and shivering with dread.

This was how Miss Beamish found them when she was on her morning walk. Once she would have run away from any emotional scene, especially something as dramatic as this. But by now she had become involved with Pepe's hopes and dreams. She sat on the chair Maria drew up for her by the fire, sipped the mint tea she had brought her, and joined in the wait.

'She'll be all right,' said Pepe. 'Jesus will make her better.'

He was so certain, in spite of his blank look, that Miss Beamish was afraid for him. She didn't want him to lose his faith as she had done when she was about his age.

The grey of the morning was like the greyness in her heart. The greyness had been there for so many years. The warmth of Pepe's family had started to break it up, like sun piercing through heavy cloud. She didn't want it to stop.

'Oh, God,' she cried in her own heart. 'Don't let this boy down.'

They all jumped to their feet at the sight of a car

bumping its way along the beach towards them. At last! The vet! He was a bearded man who, surprised by this unusual and desperate call-out, did his best, though he said it was far too late. He injected five different things into Red but she didn't seem to notice. Pepe winced at every jab.

'I've done all I can,' said the vet after that. 'I've still got to charge you.'

He was sure she was going to die and that they wouldn't want to pay him. He told them her sickness was leptospirosis which was caught from rats. 'A good dog like this should have been vaccinated against it. I've done it now but . . .'

Pepe told the whole story of Red while his mother fetched from its hiding place all the money she had managed to save. It was just enough.

'You'll know in the next few hours,' said the vet as he got back into his car. Then he drove away.

Pepe was so tired that he went to bed, taking Red with him. His mother had to carry her. Miss Beamish went home and said she'd come back the next day for news. Maria went to bed, too, and soon The Beach Café was quiet with sleep, while a fog came down and swallowed everything in its greyness.

It was dark when Pepe woke up. At first he couldn't remember why he was in bed with his clothes on. Then it all came back.

'Red!' he cried, sitting up in alarm.

She was lying at his feet but, at his cry, she lifted her head. By now, he was out of bed and switching on the light.

'Red!' he cried again, but he need not have

feared. Just by looking at her he could tell she was better.

He jumped on the mattress and flung his arms round her. 'You're all right!' he exclaimed. 'You're all right!'

'Mama! Mama!' he shouted next, running to wake her up. 'Red's better. She's well. Jesus has made her better.'

They hugged each other and then Pepe went back to hug Red again. She licked his face and made him laugh. Soon she was on all fours, weak and wobbly, but very much alive.

The days and weeks flew by. Pepe marked them off on his dog calendar and bit by bit the time for his father's return drew nearer.

Every Saturday, he told his father on the phone about the different things that Red was learning to do. She sat when told to sit. She helped collect firewood and was very good at carrying bits home between her jaws. She had such a good sense of smell that, wherever he hid anything, she could always find it. She still hadn't learnt to jump through the hoop, but sooner or later, she'd understand because she was so very clever.

Big Pepe phoned them from Madrid from time to time. He told them about his job. He was kept very busy. Not only was he making millions of Angels' Wings. He was also experimenting with all kinds of new ideas. His boss was very pleased with him.

Maria said, 'Perhaps it was right for him to go. He sounds very happy. Perhaps I was wrong.'

She said it as if she didn't altogether believe it

but it made Pepe happy. It meant she was giving up being angry with his brother.

Big Pepe sent them some postcard views of the city. Pepe pinned them up in the café next to the sketches of Madge and Red, where he could see them from his bed in the corner. Big Pepe also sent a money order to pay for the vet. They were very pleased about that because the vet's bill had taken all their money.

No matter how fresh and windy it might be, no matter how stormy the sky, there were few days when Miss Beamish didn't come for her tea. She and Maria were learning to understand each other and Maria was no longer too shy to try to talk to her.

'*Tu feliz cuando José volver,*' (You happy when José come back.) Miss Beamish said. Her Spanish, though jerky, was slowly improving.

Maria nodded. Her big smile was just like Pepe's. Miss Beamish knew she would be happy too. She had missed him all these months. How strange! She had never missed anyone before. She had wasted so many years!

At last, one Saturday afternoon, José told them he would be home the following weekend. He was going to spend one night in Madrid with Big Pepe to find out how he was getting on.

'Then, God willing, I'll be on the bus that gets in at midday. Be at the bus-stop. And bring the dog with you,' he told Pepe. 'I want to see all of you just as soon as I arrive.'

Pepe told Red over and over again about his father. He didn't want her to think he was a stranger to be growled at. 'He'll love you as much as I do,' he said, 'and you've got to love him, too. He would have given you to me if he'd found you first. Only he had to go away and the Englishman found you instead.'

It was spring now. There had still hardly been more than a shower of rain and the sun was already hot. Miss Beamish now had a morning swim, as well as a walk and both Pepe and his mother thought she was a little mad. Nobody swam before May or June. The sea was so cold. Even Red only let her paws get wet. She might be an Irish Setter but she was a very Spanish dog.

It seemed to Pepe as if Saturday would never come. He didn't care how early they got to the bus-stop. He would have gone just as soon as he jumped out of bed but his mother said it was too early.

'Is it too early now?' he asked as soon as he'd finished his breakfast.

'Is it still too early?' he asked when he'd helped put away the bedclothes and the mattress.

In the end, he and Red went on their own to the bus-stop. Maria said she'd come along later. The bus-stop was near the pine wood where Red had been found. Pepe and she explored it together. He found a teaspoon which he thought was real silver and Red poked her nose into all the dirty bags within reach.

'Do you remember being here?' Pepe asked her, wondering yet again at her miraculous appearance. Had she been dumped? Had she got lost? Why had she stayed there instead of going into the town? There were no answers to these questions except to say, 'It was a miracle, God's way of answering prayer.'

They went back to the bus-stop and sat contentedly together until Maria came along. She was wearing her best dress and had put on all her rings and bracelets. Pepe thought she was the most beautiful mother in the world.

Suddenly, the bus came into sight and Pepe could hardly wait for it to cover the last few hundred metres. He and Red were dancing about together, he waving his arms, she her tail, long before José could possibly see them. But when the bus stopped and its eight passengers got off, José wasn't among them.

'What's happened to my father?' Pepe asked the driver. 'He said he'd be on this bus.'

'How should I know?' replied the driver. 'I don't know who your father is. Perhaps he came too late.'

Maria went into a long description of what her husband looked like, hoping the driver might have seen him at the bus station.

'Lady,' said the driver somewhat impatiently. 'There are a thousand people at the bus station and half of them look like your husband. I just drive the bus.'

It was hard to take in that now they wouldn't see him till Monday because there weren't any buses on Sunday. Pepe felt like crying. Maria was worried. If José had missed the bus there must have been a good reason for it. Was something wrong with Big Pepe in Madrid?

At the Sunday meeting, the telephonist told Maria that Big Pepe had phoned. He had waited and waited at the bus station in Madrid but his father hadn't turned up. He wanted her to phone him and let him know if he'd changed his mind about meeting him and had gone straight home.

Now all the church was anxious. Maria began to moan and say, 'Something's happened to him. I know it has.'

Pepe began to feel sick with fear. He was glad when the pastor said, 'We'll all pray for him. The Lord knows where he is and why he missed the bus. Let's ask him to bring our brother safely home.'

They really expected him to come on the Monday bus. Pepe didn't want to go to school. He couldn't bear to wait till home-time to see his father. Maria gave way. She was glad of his company. Red gambolled ahead of them and again Pepe's heart filled with pride. He longed for his father to see her. He wanted to hear all he'd have to say.

There were only three people on the Monday bus and José wasn't one of them. It was the same on Tuesday. By now, Miss Beamish also knew that José hadn't returned. For the first time The Beach Café was closed, even for her. She was blank with dismay. The closed door, and Red whining mournfully inside, all alone, sent a stab of desolation through her.

It was a pain she knew well, from her childhood days at the orphanage. The doors of family life had never been open for her. She had pretended not to care. She had hardened her heart and told both the world and herself that she didn't need anybody, she didn't want anybody. She had come to Spain to spend her retirement years away from the damp and cold of her own country. Now she knew it wasn't sunshine she needed but love. The shut door of The Beach Café brought it all back and made it very clear.

For the first time in many years she felt a stab of pain in her heart, a tightness in her throat and a pricking of tears in her eyes. She felt small and helpless again, as if she were still that little girl, desperately wanting someone to want her.

She remembered the God who had failed her all those years ago, who hadn't answered her prayers. Was he the same God that this family believed in? There was only one God, so he had to be the same.

She sat at a table, staring at the sea which was calm and as blue as the sky. There was such a struggle in her heart and mind that she hardly saw it.

Everything about José and his family spoke of a loving God who knew all that was going on in their lives and cared, even about the little things. He must know where José was, what had happened to him. She didn't expect José's God to listen to her. But why did he make it so difficult for her to understand him?

If something dreadful had happened to José – if he never came back – would Maria, Big Pepe and Pepe go on loving and believing in him? Would they still talk about miracles? If José didn't come back, would The Beach Café never open its door again? Would there be no more joy and love?

'Oh, God,' she cried in her heart. 'I couldn't bear it. Not now. I'm too old. Even if you don't listen to my prayers, please listen to theirs. Bring José back home. Watch over him wherever he is. I'll forgive you for not answering my prayers before if only you'll answer them now.'

When she went home she sat down and wrote a letter to the bookshop in England that had agreed to send her any books she asked for. She asked them to send her a Bible. She wanted to find out who God was because she really didn't know.

Chapter eleven

Pepe was lying on his back looking at the night sky. Beneath him was the tough grass that, in spite of salty air and lack of rain, somehow managed to thinly carpet the sandy coastline above the beach. Red was with him. Her nose was busy, snuffling the ground within reach, but her gaze never strayed for more than a moment from the boy she loved.

Pepe hadn't come to this spot to look at the stars. He had been running, walking, running – he didn't know for how long. It hadn't been dark when he'd set out, his heart raging with fear and hurt and anger. But suddenly night had come. Blackness was all around him as well as inside him.

But he had kept going. It was the only way to keep him from exploding. It was as if there were a bomb inside him, about to go off. He hadn't wanted Red with him and had done all he could to drive her away.

At first, she'd thought he was playing a new game and she replied to his angry commands with excited barks. When he threw things at her she picked them up and tried dropping them at his feet. But he didn't react in the expected way.

She began to sense the strange anger in his shouts. Even when she did get the message – after he'd flung a bottle which hit her hard in the ribs – she wouldn't desert him. She kept warily at a distance, giving occasional yelps as if to say, 'I can't understand you but I'm not giving up.' When Pepe went on ignoring her she acted as if she were on a walk of her own and just happened to be going in the same direction.

The coastline looked high and forbidding in the darkness. It was just what Pepe needed at that moment, something to fight with, something solid and real that he could challenge and defeat. The moonlight hindered his struggle, throwing shadows in all the wrong places. But the feel of the rough earth, and the concentration he needed, calmed the rage in his heart.

He panted and trembled and threw himself down. Then the torrent broke. He sobbed and sobbed as if he'd never be able to stop, beating the ground with his fists.

He was sobbing out all the agony of the last two weeks – the waiting, hoping, believing, until the cruel fact had to be faced. After setting out for the overnight journey to Madrid, his father had disappeared. No one knew how or when or why or where. He had just vanished, along with his tool-kit, his bag of clothes and the money he'd been paid for his work.

Everything that could be done to trace him had been done. The police had checked all the hospitals and reported accidents. They even checked to see if he'd been arrested. Every day, Maria went to the station to ask for news but it was always the same. Nothing!

The church met every night to pray for him and the family. Maria was comforted and given hope for each new day. But she had stopped saying to Pepe, 'Perhaps tomorrow . . .' He didn't know whether that was good or bad. Every day, he couldn't help hoping as he came out of school that his father would be there. But every day the disappointment, when he wasn't there, made him feel sick and crushed.

Then Big Pepe said he would come home and a great load lifted from Pepe's heart. Surely his brother would know what to do. Surely, with him at home once more, it wouldn't be so bad. He told himself that if Big Pepe came home his father would come home too. They would be a family again and everything would be as it used to be. His broken world would be put back together again.

When they met Big Pepe at the bus-stop, he couldn't help bursting into tears. He wanted his father to be on the bus also. Maria cried too and while Big Pepe put his arms round them both, Red whimpered and pawed at Pepe, confused by so much emotion.

Maria told Big Pepe the whole story all over again, though he knew it. He told them all that he had done in Madrid to find his father, though they knew that, too. And a horrible thudding panic rose in Pepe's heart as he listened because everything was the same. Big Pepe's coming wasn't going to change anything.

His brother was like a stranger to him. He didn't say or do any of the things Pepe expected. Instead of being strong and full of ideas, he sat in a corner of the café with his head in his hands and began to sob. Between sobs, words blurted out jerkily.

'When I was a boy I was always scared he wouldn't come back. Every time he went away . . . I was afraid. I knew that one day he wouldn't come back . . . And now it's happened. It's my fault. I shouldn't have gone away. He didn't want me to go until he came back . . .'

Pepe couldn't bear any more. He vaguely saw his mother pulling Big Pepe into her arms, tears running down her own cheeks, but he had to get away . . .

Red found it much harder to get up the sandy rock-face. She'd run back and forth at its base, barking for Pepe to come back or to wait for her. When he didn't, she found her own way up further along.

Pepe's sobs drew her to where he was. She whined and flattened her ears and circled round him, afraid of his stormy pain. Then she dropped down at a distance and waited. As the crying slowed and stopped she crept nearer, bit by bit, ready to dash out of reach again.

She saw him roll on to his back. She sensed that the rage was over. With a little whine of hope, she crept right up to him. He stretched out a hand. This made her go wild with joy. She galloped round in circles, dashing up to him, dashing away again, each time giving his fingers a lick. Then she calmed down and flopped beside him, long tongue dripping as she panted and waited.

There was something about the stars that brought peace to Pepe's heart. Why were they there? Why were there so many? He'd never really looked at them although they'd been his ceiling many a summer night.

The memory of something the pastor had read, when he'd come to talk and pray with them, came to his mind. It had to do with God being on a throne, high above the earth – higher than the stars that were so far away and yet seemed so close. And it had to do with people being like grasshoppers.

Pepe knew about grasshoppers. Many a time he caught them, just to see how high and how far they'd jump when he let them go. He'd never thought that, to God, he was like a grasshopper. But he felt like one when he looked at the stars.

God was so big, the pastor said. It was impossible to understand him. He made the stars and he made the grasshoppers and nobody could really know why. Nor could anyone know why God let bad things happen.

'The wonderful thing is,' Pepe remembered him saying, 'that God can make good things come out of the bad.'

That didn't make sense to Pepe. Then he'd said, 'You can only see the stars in the dark. We're all in the dark right now over what's happened, but we have to trust God. When we can't see where we're going, we need to hold his hand.'

Pepe had once asked his father if he was ever scared when he was working on high scaffolding. And his father had laughed and said, 'I don't need to be scared because the Lord is always holding on to my shirt.'

Surely he'd be holding on to his father's shirt right now, wherever he was, and one day he'd bring him home.

Big Pepe only stayed for a few days. There was nothing he could do, except repair the thatch and fix up the coloured lights for the new season. Maria told him he must go back to Madrid.

'The Lord has given you that job. I was wrong when I wanted to stop you. Where else will the money come from to keep us going? And I want your father to be proud of you when he does come back. Pepe and I will look after things here and one day, God willing, something good will come out of all this.'

'I don't believe in God any more,' said Big Pepe.

'Then why are you so angry with him?'

For the first time Big Pepe laughed.

The night before he left, Pepe asked him to read the story of the lost sheep again.

'I like that story,' he said. 'It reminds me of how Jesus brought Red to us. No one knew where she was except Jesus and he knows where Papa is. He'll make someone find him and bring him home.'

Big Pepe hadn't looked at the Bible since he'd gone away. After he'd read the story, he was silent for a long time. He couldn't stare into the fire because it was too warm for fires, but he had a far-away look which Pepe didn't like.

'Say something,' he demanded, 'just like Papa used to.'

'Yes,' agreed Maria. 'Tell us something.'

'I was thinking I've been like that silly sheep that wandered away, that didn't want to stay where it was safe. I didn't want to join the church in Madrid. I didn't want to read the Bible or pray. I wanted to go my own way, live my own life. My heart was growing cold and hard . . .'

Pepe could hear the tremble in his brother's voice as he went on, 'If nothing had happened to Papa, if I hadn't had to come back . . .'

He couldn't say any more.

Maria said, 'We have a very strange but wonderful God who does make good things come out of bad. It says so in his word. We have only to believe it.'

She began to sing:

'What a good God we have,
Who has given us hope,
Who has made us in his image and likeness.
I will praise the God who made me
Who has made me as strong as a rock.'

They sang it together, over and over, and for the first time since his father had disappeared, Pepe started to feel hope in his heart once more.

Chapter twelve

The hope didn't go away, not even when they had to say goodbye to Big Pepe again. Every time Pepe looked at Red, he knew it was right to have hope. But it was very hard.

The weeks went by and the holiday-makers started to arrive. Red had to be tied up while Pepe was serving customers. Otherwise she would have been under his feet all day. She hated it and so did Pepe. Maria had hired a man to do his father's job, but helping him wasn't the same as helping his father. He'd rather be with Red.

When he complained his mother said, 'When your father comes back, won't he want to see everything as it was before?'

'But Red doesn't like being tied up.'

'Red has to learn she can't always do what she wants, any more than we can.'

Tired and angry, he burst out, 'What if Papa never comes back?'

'He will. I just know it in my heart. He will come back,' she said.

'Do you know it the same way I knew it about Red?' he asked.

'Yes,' she said and folded him into her arms.

Pepe thought about his mother's words in the night, when it was too hot for sleeping even though he was too tired to stay awake. He thought about the miracle that had brought him Red. What would have happened if he'd given up believing and had taken an Airedale puppy instead? Would he have still got Red? He didn't know. There were some things you just couldn't know.

The thoughts swirled round in his mind, mingling with memories and prayers and different things people said. In his thoughts, or in his dreams (because on hot nights you could never really know if you were awake or asleep), he could see his father coming home. Walking down the road from the bus-stop. Looking very tired. But coming home.

It was such a vivid thought – or dream – that Pepe could hardly live with it. Every day he wanted to go to the bus-stop and wait for the bus, certain that one day his dream would come true.

He told his mother. She didn't laugh at him. She pressed him close in her arms and said, 'That's how it will be one day. I'm sure.'

'Then let me go with Red and wait for him,' he begged.

'But there are three buses a day now. You can't go and meet every one. I need you here. You know that.'

Pepe couldn't make her understand, but it made work harder. He'd keep wondering if his father was walking down the road, disappointed because no one had come to meet him. He kept looking along the beach, straining his dark eyes against the sun's glare. Although there were so many people, he'd recognise his father at once. He wouldn't look like a holiday-maker. He'd have his tool-kit and his bag.

Big Pepe came back for the month of August. Everyone in Madrid had gone away to the mountains or the sea. He did the cooking at home instead and found time to go swimming with Pepe and Red. When all the customers were gone, and a cool breeze came in from the sea, he read the Bible to them as José used to. The stars gleamed down and everything was quiet and almost as it used to be.

'Do you believe Papa will come home?' Pepe asked him one night.

Big Pepe didn't answer for a while. Then he said slowly, 'I don't know what's happened to him, why – if he's alive – he hasn't phoned or anything. But one thing I am sure of. If something's stopping him, God will sort it out. And when he's able to come, nothing will stop him.'

'Do you think he is alive?' asked Pepe. He couldn't believe anything else – didn't want to believe anything else – and yet . . . why didn't he come?

'He's alive somewhere,' said Big Pepe. 'Whether in heaven or on earth, I don't know. But we'll see him again one day. I'm sure of that.'

'I want to see him now,' said Pepe. 'I want him to come home. I don't want to wait till I go to heaven. I want him to see Red.'

Big Pepe laughed. 'How long would you have waited for Red?' he asked.

'For ever!' came the immediate reply.

'Then don't give up. Leave it with the Lord. He has a right time for everything.'

August came to an end. Before returning to Madrid Big Pepe took his brother to the shop to buy his new school books. Last year – Pepe had gone with his father and they had looked through them together afterwards.

'You kids today are so clever!' he had exclaimed, scratching his head at everything Pepe would be learning that year. Big Pepe didn't do things like that. He just told him to make sure he got good marks in all his exams.

His mother looked at the pictures but the words meant nothing. Pepe offered to teach her to read but she shook her head. 'All those squiggles make my eyes spin.'

By October the town was back to one bus each day and Pepe remembered his dream. It came back to him as if he'd only just dreamt it. It was so real again that, instead of going to school, he hung about near the bus-stop, certain his father would come. As the bus came into sight his heart began to throb and his face burned. But his father wasn't on the bus and he felt sick with disappointment.

Perhaps he'd just got the day wrong! So he went again the next day and the day after that, each time more and more certain that his dream would come true. Even though he was wrong each time he kept going. It was something he just had to do.

After a fortnight, his teacher came to find out why he was missing school. His mother was very angry until he told her what he was doing.

'Going to the bus-stop every day won't bring him back,' she tried to explain. 'Do you think he'd want you to be missing school like this?'

Pepe couldn't speak. He looked down, not wanting the teacher to see his eyes filled with tears. He knew they felt sorry for him, but they didn't understand.

'Promise me you won't miss school again,' demanded his mother.

This was too much to ask. He shook his head.

'But, Pepe, you can't go waiting at the bus-stop every day. You've got to go to school.'

'It's been two weeks,' reminded the teacher. 'You'll have to see the headmaster if you refuse to attend classes.'

'He'll go to school,' said Maria firmly. 'I'll talk to him.'

She did. She said she would go to the bus-stop in his place and that they could go together on Saturdays.

But José didn't come on the bus when he came. He was given a lift by a truck driver who saw him limping along the deserted road at dusk, about ten kilometres from the town. There was no one at the bus-stop where the driver dropped him off, and the November darkness was only broken when clouds gave way to the moon. But José knew the road and by the time the rough beach was beneath his feet he could already see The Beach Café outlined by leaping firelight.

Pepe was carefully pushing broken planks into the flames while Red trotted here and there with waving tail, picking up bits and dropping them, being helpful in her own way. All of a sudden, she became aware of the man on the beach in the darkness. She went stiff with curiosity, one paw lifted, muzzle high to catch the stranger's scent.

'What's the matter, Red?' asked Pepe.

Even as he spoke, *he knew*! Giving a loud cry, he threw down the wood in his hands and ran towards the figure he could hardly see.

'*Papa!*'

Red loped along beside him. Soon she was ahead, but she ran wide of the stranger as she saw Pepe throw himself into his outstretched arms with wild sobs. She flattened her ears at the sound, then pricked them again. They weren't like the sobs she'd heard on the hill.

Soon she was willing to let this stranger touch her, as Pepe called her to him and said, 'Red, this is my father. I've already told you about him. Now he's come home.'

The next few days were a confused whirl of laughter, tears, joy and questions. But José could give no explanations. Both his speech and memory were confused. The doctor thought he might have had a stroke. He said he must see a specialist. He also said it might be a long time before José could tell them about the missing months of his life, if he could ever remember them.

The important thing was that somehow he had found his way home, penniless and wearing clothes that were not his own. Although he couldn't answer their questions, he was back where he belonged and his smile was the same.

No one could wait till Sunday for a time of special thanksgiving, so the whole church went

94

along to The Beach Café to welcome José back and to praise the Lord who had looked after him on the way. Big Pepe arrived from Madrid just in time and, of course, Miss Beamish couldn't be left out.

A huge fire was built that evening, around which they sat and gave thanks to God. As the flames lit up the different faces in the darkness – all shining with joy – Miss Beamish remembered a verse she had read in the Bible that had been sent from England.

' "I am the light of the world . . . Whoever follows me will have the light of life and will never walk in the darkness." '

Jesus had said that, more than once. They were all still in the dark as to what had happened to José. But one thing was sure – Jesus had been his light and had brought him home.

She suddenly knew that this was the light she needed, the home she had always been shut out from. She didn't need to be in the dark any longer! The tears that began to slide down her cheeks were not only tears of joy for José's home-coming but also for her own.

Pepe sat at his father's feet, leaning against him with face aglow. Red was beside him and the firelight made her coat look like burnished bronze. She was so beautiful and she was behaving perfectly, in spite of all the noise and excitement.

She kept looking up at Pepe, sensing his joy. And Pepe kept looking up at his father, still hardly able to believe that he was really there and that he wasn't dreaming.